W9-AVI-680

THE BIGGEST, BEST SNOWMAN

6400623

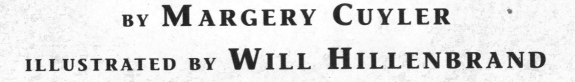

BY **MARGERY CUYLER**
ILLUSTRATED BY **WILL HILLENBRAND**

SCHOLASTIC PRESS

NEW YORK

Text copyright © 1998 by Margery Cuyler
Illustrations copyright © 1998 by Will Hillenbrand
All rights reserved. Published by Scholastic Press, a division of Scholastic Inc., *Publishers since 1920.*
SCHOLASTIC and SCHOLASTIC PRESS and associated logos are trademarks and/or registered trademarks of Scholastic Inc.

No part of this publication may be reproduced, or stored in a retrieval system, or transmitted in any form or by any means,
electronic, mechanical, photocopying, recording, or otherwise, without written permission of the publisher. For information
regarding permissions, write to Scholastic Inc., Attention: Permissions Department, 555 Broadway, New York, NY 10012.

Library of Congress Cataloging-in-Publication Data
Cuyler, Margery.
The biggest, best snowman / by Margery Cuyler : illustrated by Will Hillenbrand. — 1st ed.   p.   cm.
Summary: Little Nell is told by her BIG sisters and her mother that she is too small to help out, but everyone, including Nell,
feels differently after her forest friends give her the confidence to build a large snowman.
ISBN 0-590-13922-3
[1. Size — Fiction. 2. Self-confidence — Fiction. 3. Animals — Fiction. 4. Snow — Fiction.] I. Hillenbrand, Will, ill. II. Title.
PZ7.C997Bi 1998 97-36720 [E] — dc21 CIP AC

10 9 8 7 6 5 4 3 2 1   8 9/9 0/0 01 02 03
Printed in Mexico 49
First edition, November 1998
The illustrations for this book were created on vellum using oils, oil pastel,
egg tempera, watercolors, water-soluble artist crayons, and pencil.
The type for this book was set in Stone Informal.
Design by Will Hillenbrand and Becky Terhune

For Will Hillenbrand, with thanks for the Christmas card
that inspired this story, and for Carol Vukelich. — M. C.

For Ian my son, Jane my wife, and a BIG November snow,
my inspiration. — W. H.

Little Nell lived with BIG Mama, BIG Sarah, and BIG Lizzie in a BIG house in a BIG snowy woods.

BIG Mama, BIG Sarah, and BIG Lizzie had BIG blustery voices. They had BIG talky friends. They had BIG loud parties. When Little Nell asked, "Can I help?" BIG Mama, BIG Sarah, and BIG Lizzie shook their heads. "No, you can't," they said. "You're too small."

"Yes, I can," said Little Nell,
"and no, I'm not."
"No, you can't," they said,
"and yes, you are!"

So Little Nell would go into the BIG snowy woods. She would sit and watch the snow fall from the sky. She would walk under the bare-branched trees. She would play with her friends, Reindeer, Hare, and Bear Cub.

One day, Bear Cub said to Little Nell, "Can you show us how to make a snowman?"

"No, I can't," said Little Nell. "I'm too small."

"Yes, you can," said the animals, "and no, you're not!"

"But I'm so small," said Little Nell, "my family won't let me do anything. I could never make a snowman."

"How do you know unless you try?" asked Bear Cub. "We'll help you."

Little Nell sighed. "Well, maybe," she said.

Little Nell got down on her knees.
She carefully patted and matted and
batted the snow into a tiny ball.

She rolled it and rolled it and rolled
it to Reindeer. Reindeer nudged it and
nudged it and nudged it to Hare.

Hare kicked it and kicked it and
kicked it to Bear Cub.

Bear Cub rolled it and rolled it and
rolled it until it stopped — THUD —
by the edge of a BIG icy pond.

"Now what?" asked Reindeer.

"The snowman needs a middle," said Little Nell.

"How do we do that?" asked Hare.

Little Nell bit her lip. She got down on her knees. She carefully patted and matted and batted another tiny snowball.

She rolled it and rolled it to Reindeer. Reindeer nudged it and nudged it to Hare. Hare kicked it and kicked it to Bear Cub.

Bear Cub rolled it and rolled it
until — THUD — it came to a stop.
He pushed it on top of the other
snowball.

"Now what?" he asked.

"It needs a head!" cried Little Nell.
She patted and matted and batted
another tiny snowball. Then she rolled
it to Reindeer. Reindeer nudged it to
Hare. Hare kicked it to Bear Cub.

Bear Cub stuck it on top
of the other two snowballs.

Little Nell and the animals stood back and looked at their snowman.

"Something's missing," said Hare.

"The face," said Little Nell.

"How do we do that?" asked the animals.

"I think we'll need help," said Little Nell.

She whistled for the birds to come. Crow, Cardinal, and Sparrow flew down from the trees.

"Could you make a face for our snowman?" she asked.

Crow fetched two pieces of bark for the eyes.

Cardinal found an old pink sock for the nose.

Sparrow brought raisins for the mouth.

Little Nell handed her green scarf to the birds. They wound it and wound it and wound it around the snowman's neck. Then they added two sticks for arms.

The snowman was finally finished.

Little Nell and the animals gazed up at their creation.

"Wow!" said the animals.

"Wow!" said Little Nell.

It was almost lunchtime. Little
Nell said good-bye to her friends.
She walked home through the
BIG snowy woods.

BIG Mama, BIG Sarah, and BIG Lizzie were waiting for her.

"Where have you been?" they asked in their BIG blustery voices.

"I was building a great big snowman," answered Little Nell.

"How could someone as little as you build a great BIG snowman?" asked BIG Lizzie.

"Come and see," said Little Nell.

So BIG Mama, BIG Sarah, and BIG
Lizzie followed Little Nell through the
BIG snowy woods to the snowman.

As they looked up, their mouths dropped open and their arms dropped to their sides.

"Wow!" they said. "You built that?"

"Yes, I did," said Little Nell, "with the help of my friends."

"That is the biggest, best snowman that ever was," said BIG Mama.

"Yes, it is," said Little Nell, a huge smile on her face.

"Will you come and help us make a BIG yummy lunch?"
asked BIG Sarah.

"No, she can't," said BIG Lizzie. "She's still too small."

"Yes, I can," said Little Nell, "and no, I'm not!"

"Yes, you can," said BIG Mama, "and yes, you WILL!"

BIG Mama gave Little Nell a BIG sloppy kiss — SMOOCH!
BIG Sarah gave Little Nell a BIG squeezy hug — OOCH!
BIG Lizzie stuck her BIG nose in the air — HMMPH!

Little Nell's friends lifted her
to the top of the snowman —

98132

LIBRARY
JEFFERSON LINCOLN SCHOOL
CENTRALIA, WA. 98531

DATE DUE

MAR 05	DEC 10	DEC 09
MAR 19	MAY 03	NOV 16
NOV 16	DEC 09	
MAR 08	FEB 06	
MAY 25	MAR 03	
JUN 04	JAN 12	
DEC 05	FEB 09	

E   98132
Cuy

Cuyler, Margery
The Biggest, Best Snowman

          $15.95

Lexile: 480